# Disney's Doug™

Created by
Jim Jinkins

# Twelve Days
of Christmas

Original characters for "The Funnies" developed by Jim Jinkins and Joe Aaron.

Copyright © 1998 by Disney Enterprises, Inc.

Printed in Singapore.

First Edition
1 3 5 7 9 10 8 6 4 2

The artwork for this book is prepared using watercolor.
The text for this book is set in 18-point New Century Schoolbook.

Library of Congress Catalog Card Number: 97-49654

ISBN: 0-7868-3197-9

Disney's

# Doug™

Created by
Jim Jinkins

# Twelve Days
of Christmas

JUMBO
PICTURES
INC.

GRADE A QUALITY

Story by Linda K. Garvey
Illustrated by Matthew C. Peters, Jeffrey Nodelman, Tim Chi Ly, Vinh Troong, Tony Curanaj, Brian Donnelly

Disney
PRESS

NEW YORK

It was the morning of Christmas Eve, and Doug couldn't think of what to give Patti Mayonnaise for Christmas. After all, she was perfect so her gift had to be perfect!

He thought he could make Hamlet, Patti's pet guinea pig, a maze.

But then Hamlet had gotten lost and Patti was worried.

Now the maze was a bogus idea and he was almost out of time . . .

. . . and money!

Four dollars and eighty-three cents was not enough to buy the most perfect girl in the universe the most perfect present ever!

"Porkchop," he said to his best nonhuman friend, "I don't suppose I could borrow . . . ?"

Porkchop stood up to pull empty pockets out of his fur.

". . . Three French hens, two turtledoves, and a partridge in a pear tree!" warbled the Liver City Singers on K-BLUF.

"Man," Doug told Porkchop, "I'd be happy to have just one good present for Patti!" His eyes glazed over and his mind began to drift.

On the first day of Christmas,
Doug Funnie gave to me a Porkchop in a goatee.

On the second day of Christmas,
Doug Funnie gave to me Two Neematoads

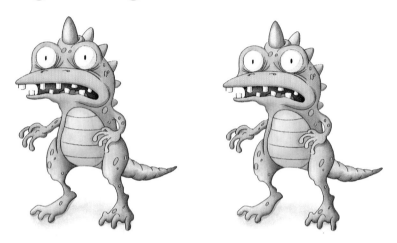

and a Porkchop in a goatee.

On the third day of Christmas,
Doug Funnie gave to me Three Wacky Wizzers

2 Neematoads

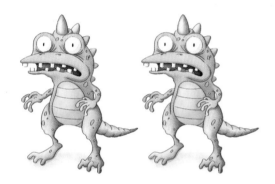

and a Porkchop in a goatee.

"You can't give Porkchop away! Are you crazy?"

"But it rhymes! Sort of."

On the fourth day of Christmas,
Doug Funnie gave to me Four AV nerds,

---

**3** Wacky Wizzers

and a Porkchop in a goatee.

**2** Neematoads

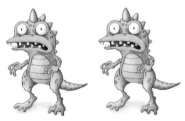

On the fifth day of Christmas,

Doug Funnie gave to me Five broken things!

---

**4** AV nerds

**3** Wacky Wizzers

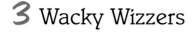

**2** Neematoads

and a Porkchop in a goatee.

"Porkchop and partridge? Hah!"

"What do you expect? I'm a knight, not a poet!"

On the sixth day of Christmas,
Doug Funnie gave to me Six Dink-y gadgets,

**5** broken things!

**2** Neematoads

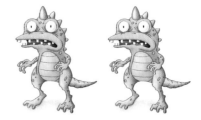

**4** AV nerds

and a Porkchop in a goatee.

**3** Wacky Wizzers

On the seventh day of Christmas,

Doug Funnie gave to me  Seven Tater Twisties,

**6** Dink-y gadgets

**5** broken things!

**4** AV nerds

**3** Wacky Wizzers

**2** Neematoads

and a Porkchop in a goatee.

"Well, you can't give
Porkchop away."

"Yeah, but he's
the best one!"

On the eighth day of Christmas,

Doug Funnie gave to me Eight cows a-mooing,

---

**7** Tater Twisties

**6** Dink-y gadgets

**5** broken things!

**4** AV nerds

**3** Wacky Wizzers

**2** Neematoads

and a Porkchop in a goatee.

On the ninth day of Christmas,

Doug Funnie gave to me Nine Yaks a-clogging,

**8** cows a-mooing

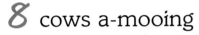

**7** Tater Twisties

**6** Dink-y gadgets

**5** broken things!

**4** AV nerds

**3** Wacky Wizzers

**2** Neematoads

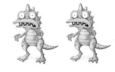

and a Porkchop
in a goatee.

"Of course! He's Porkchop! Find something else."

"How about 'A Beet-ba-all Ca-a-ad-dy?'"

On the tenth day of Christmas,
Doug Funnie gave to me Ten power briefs a-charging,

**9** Yaks a-clogging

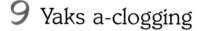

**8** cows a-mooing

**7** Tater Twisties

**6** Dink-y gadgets

**5** broken things!

**4** AV nerds

**3** Wacky Wizzers

**2** Neematoads

and a Porkchop in a goatee.

On the eleventh day of Christmas,

Doug Funnie gave to me, Eleven yodeling trophies,

**10** power briefs a-charging

**9** Yaks a-clogging

**8** cows a-mooing

**7** Tater Twisties

**6** Dink-y gadgets

**5** broken things!

**4** AV nerds

**3** Wacky Wizzers

**2** Neematoads

and a Porkchop
in a goatee.

"We did that already."

"Think of some-
thing! Quick!"

On the twelfth day of Christmas,
Doug Funnie gave to me Twelve Frothy Goats,

**11** yodeling trophies

**10** power briefs
a-charging

**9** Yaks a-clogging

**8** cows a-mooing

**7** Tater Twisties

**6** Dink-y gadgets

**5** broken things!

**4** AV nerds

**3** Wacky Wizzers

**2** Neematoads

"Goats!
I got it!"

And a Hamlet eating goat cheese!

As the song ended, Doug snapped out of his daydream.
Doug patted Porkchop. "Come on, pal! I have a brilliant
idea!"

Doug's sister Judy called from downstairs, "Doug! Patti
Mayonnaise is here!"

Doug and Porkchop raced downstairs. Patti, holding her
ice skates, was wearing the earrings he had given her last
Christmas.

"Hey, Patti," he greeted the girl of his dreams. "Merry Christmas. Has Hamlet turned up yet?"

"No," she answered. "I hope he's all right. He's never been gone this long."

"Don't worry. I'm sure he'll come back soon," Doug reassured her.

"Thanks, Doug. But the reason I'm here is because I've been trying to think of a good Christmas present for you but nothing seems right. So I thought we could have a picnic and go skating on Lucky Duck Lake. I made some sandwiches," she said as she smiled at him.

Doug's heart soared. "Great idea!" he said. "Let me get my scarf and skates!"

As they left his house, Doug told Patti, "First, I have to go to the grocery store, and then we have to stop by your house."

"All right," she answered. "But why?"

"You'll see," he promised.

"Okay, but you're being very mysterious, Doug," she said.

Patti let them into the apartment.
Porkchop began to sniff around the room,
making odd little whiny noises. Doug broke the goat
cheese into small bits and set them all around the room.

"You've gone wacky, Doug!" Patti exclaimed. "You're putting little hunks of cheese all over my floor!"

"Just wait and see," he explained.

"Well, okay, but it seems pretty weird to me!" said Patti doubtfully.

Doug was busy watching the little chunks of cheese.

Ten minutes later, Doug was still watching the hunks of cheese. Porkchop was still prowling around the furniture. And Patti was getting impatient.

"Whatever you're doing, it's not working," she said.

"Yeah, I guess not," he agreed sadly.

Just then, a shadow flashed by the bottom of the sofa.

"Hey! I saw something!" Doug cried.

"Doug? What are you doing?" Patti asked.

Doug was crawling behind the sofa. There, nestled beneath the carpet, with a little piece of goat cheese in his mouth, stood Hamlet with six teeny baby guinea pigs!

"Oh, wow!" Doug exclaimed. "Patti, I think Hamlet's a she, not a he."

"Doug!" she squealed in pure joy. "You found him?"

"Yeah!" he said. "You gotta see *her!*"

When Patti saw Hamlet and her little brood, she was thrilled. "Wow, Doug! This is the best Christmas present ever!

"You little rascal!" she told her pet fondly. "I guess I'm going to have to call you Ophelia."

They shredded some newspaper and put some goat cheese in a cardboard box, and then put Ophelia and her new family into it.

Later, skating figure eights with Patti and Porkchop, Doug thought to himself how much fun they were having. Nothing in the world could have been a better present than this!

MERRY CHRISTMAS TO ONE AND ALL!